JAMBERRY

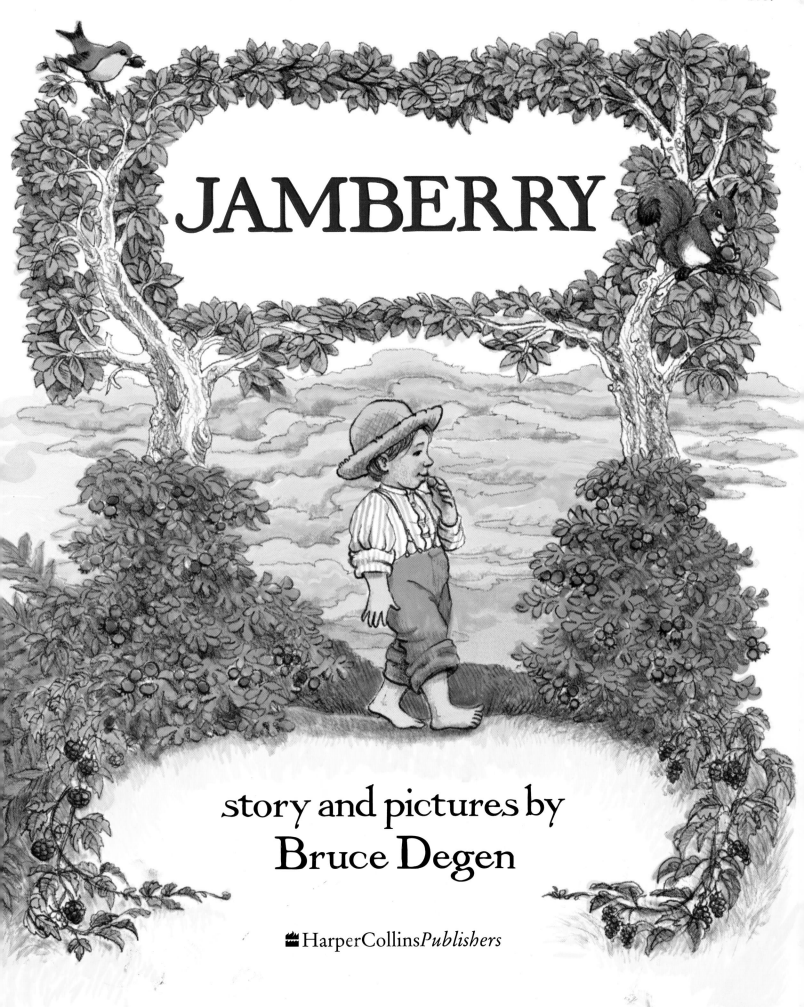

JAMBERRY

story and pictures by
Bruce Degen

HarperCollins*Publishers*

PZ8.3.D364Jam   1983   (E)

ISBN 0-06-021416-3
ISBN 0-06-021417-1 (lib. bdg.)
ISBN 0-06-443068-5 (pbk.)

82-47708

Jamberry
Copyright © 1983, 2000 by Bruce Degen
Printed in the U.S.A. All rights reserved.
http://www.harperchildrens.com

Library of Congress Cataloging-in-Publication Data
Degen, Bruce.
  Jamberry.

Summary: A little boy walking in the forest meets a big lovable bear that takes him on a delicious berry-picking
adventure in the magical world of Berryland.

  [1. Stories in rhyme.]   I. Title.

     1   2   3   4   5   6   7   8   9   10   ❖   New Edition

For my special Berry Picker
and the two Little Berries

One berry
Two berry
Pick me a blueberry

Hatberry
Shoeberry
In my canoeberry

Under the bridge
And over the dam
Looking for berries
Berries for jam

Three berry
Four berry
Hayberry
Strawberry

Finger and pawberry
My berry, your berry

Strawberry ponies
Strawberry lambs
Dancing in meadows
Of strawberry jam

Quickberry!
Quackberry!
Pick me a blackberry!

Trainberry
Trackberry
Clickety-clackberry

Rumble and ramble
In blackberry bramble
Billions of berries
For blackberry jamble

Raspberry

Jazzberry

Razzamatazzberry

Berryband

Merryband

Jamming in Berryland

Raspberry rabbits
Brassberry band
Elephants skating
On raspberry jam

Moonberry
Starberry
Cloudberry sky

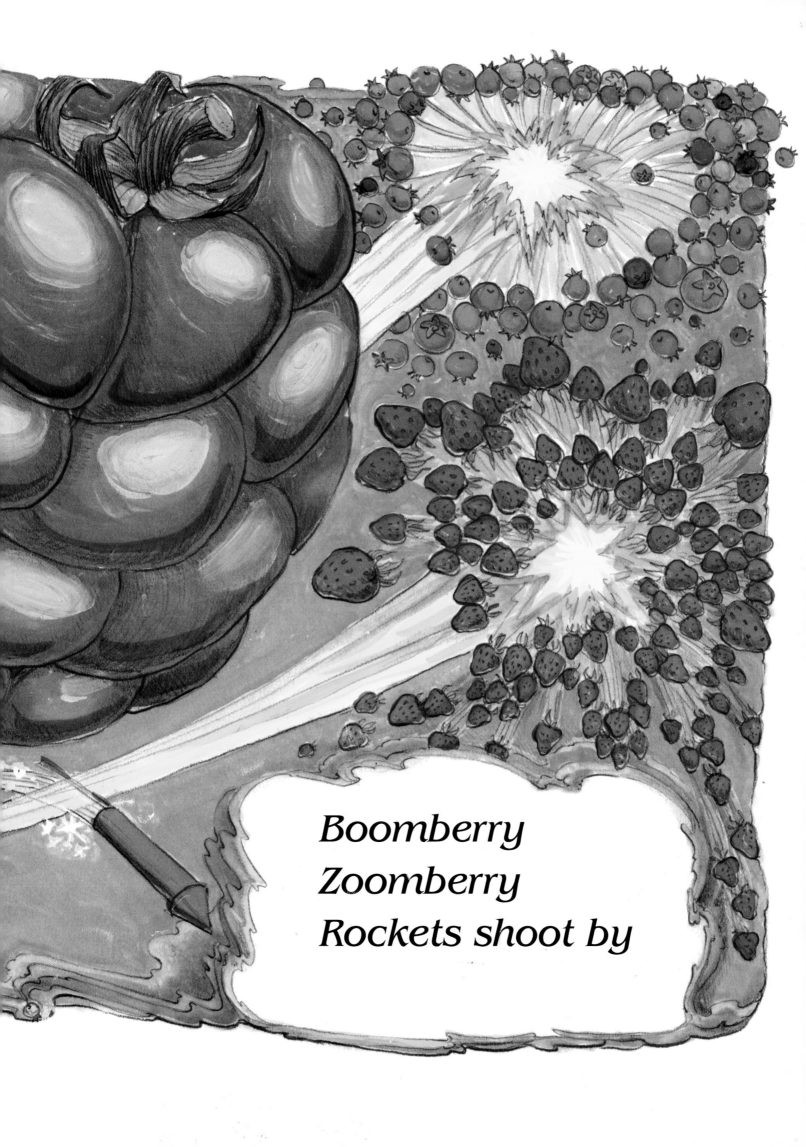

Boomberry
Zoomberry
Rockets shoot by

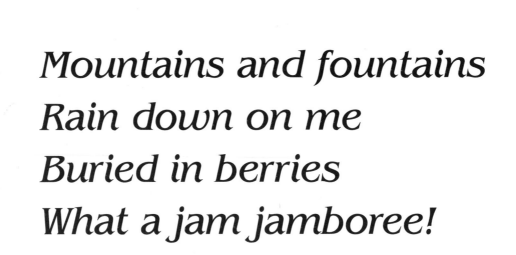

Mountains and fountains
Rain down on me
Buried in berries
What a jam jamboree!

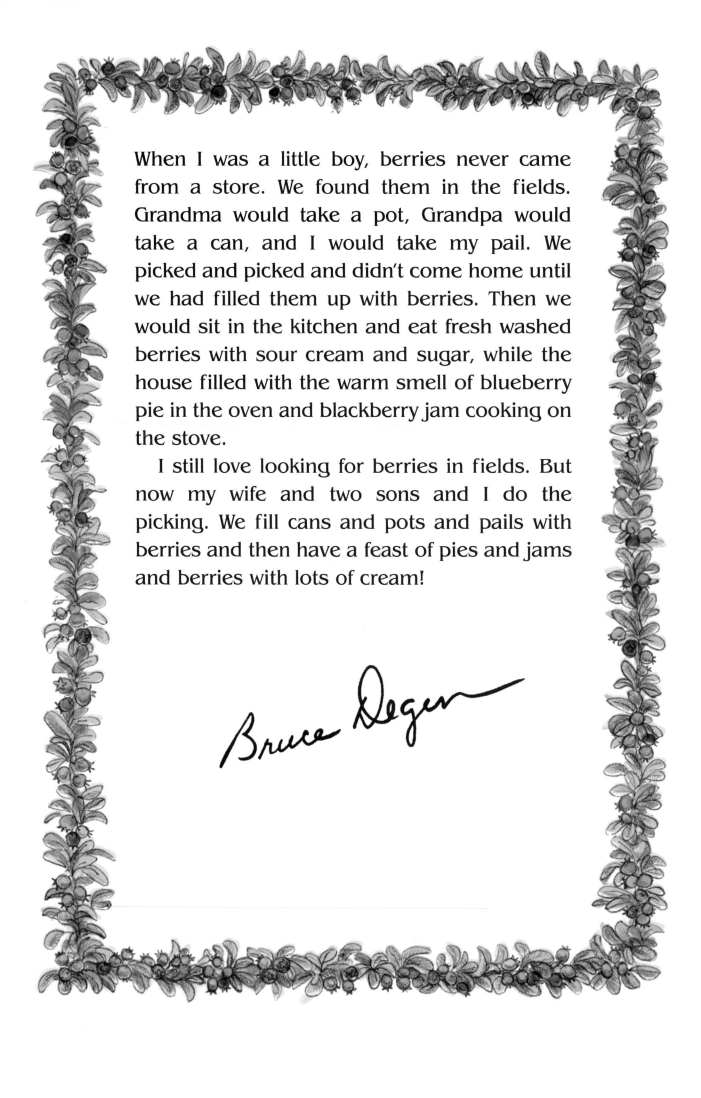

When I was a little boy, berries never came from a store. We found them in the fields. Grandma would take a pot, Grandpa would take a can, and I would take my pail. We picked and picked and didn't come home until we had filled them up with berries. Then we would sit in the kitchen and eat fresh washed berries with sour cream and sugar, while the house filled with the warm smell of blueberry pie in the oven and blackberry jam cooking on the stove.

I still love looking for berries in fields. But now my wife and two sons and I do the picking. We fill cans and pots and pails with berries and then have a feast of pies and jams and berries with lots of cream!

Bruce Degen